Mine to Worship

Veteran K9 Team

Book 6

Kameron Claire

Snuggle Whore Press, LLC

Copyright © 2021 by Kameron Claire

All rights reserved.

No part of this book may be reproduced in any form or by any electronic or mechanical means, including information storage and retrieval systems, without written permission from the author, except for the use of brief quotations in a book review.

This is a work of fiction. Names, characters, places, and incidents either are the products of the author's imagination or are used fictitiously based upon freely provided by fan submission. Any resemblance to actual persons, living or dead, businesses, companies, events, or locales is entirely coincidental.

Please respect the author and do not participate in or encourage piracy of copyrighted materials that would violate the author's rights.

Contains explicit love scenes and adult language. The suggested reading audience is 18 years or older.

Editor: Shay M Williams

Covers by SWP Covers

!! Formerly titled Codename: Bishop !!

Dedication

This series is dedicated to every individual
who signs a blank check on their ass
by enlisting in the Armed Forces
to serve their country—and to the
loved ones who support them back home.

We are Witty, Wicked & Wild wherever we go!

VETERAN
K9
TEAM
REPORTING
FOR DUTY

Prologue
Bishop

"No one wants to meet your sister—not if she looks like you." Jester chuckles and smacks Saint on the arm.

There are four of us patrolling in our tactical gear, our M-4s slung across our chests. Saint's K9, Lucifer, is sniffing the ground, alerting us to absolutely nothing. It's been quiet in this region lately—boring really—but we have six more months before we go home, and a lot can happen between now and then.

"Actually, Saint's little sister is hot," Hollywood says, looking up from the tactical tablet in his hand with a wry grin on his face. "I'm pretty sure she's adopted."

"When the fuck have you ever seen my sister?" Saint growls.

"When your dumb ass was busy admiring yourself in the mirror and left your phone unlocked. She sent a video of her dancing on top of a bar all Coyote Ugly style. It was sexy as *fuuuuuck*." Hollywood stresses the word to drive home his point.

I whistle at the same time Saint groans, "Oh shit. Who else saw the video?"

"No one, man. I wouldn't sell you out like that." Hollywood grins. "Besides, I don't want these horn dogs skeezing on my future wife."

"Never going to happen," Jester shakes his head, answering for Saint. "No self respecting grunt is going to let one of us meet his sweet single sister."

For the most part, that's true. Only these assholes don't know that I've been invited to spend next Christmas with Jester and his sister on a tropical island somewhere. My family won't be happy about it, but the idea of lounging on a white sandy beach with a drink in my hand sounds too good to pass up. Of course, he hasn't yet shown me a picture of her, so I'm positive the thought of us is an absolute no-go in his mind.

That doesn't mean I don't enjoy giving him shit. We all do it to any guy with a sister back home. It's just some-thing we do, and considering I'm an only child, I'm immune to the annoyance and therefore chief shit talker amongst us.

I chuckle. "Spoken like a guy with a hot sister back home—"

I hear before I see the bullets whiz by our heads, a chunk of concrete shattering off the corner of the building near my face.

"Take cover!" Jester shoves me to the ground before

white-hot heat shreds through my shoulder. He jumps on top of me, pinning my arms underneath my body.

"Get off me, man," I grunt.

I can't get to my gun.

Can't lift my head to see what's incoming.

Can't scramble for shelter.

Jester doesn't move.

Gunfire—a series of rata-tat-tats—sounds off next to us as Saint and Hollywood return fire from their crouched positions behind a shredded concrete wall.

I roll out from underneath my best friend and scramble to his side. Slumped over, Jester's body is limp. I pull him with my one useful arm—my other a combination of dead weight and blazing fire—a few feet behind the building we'd just passed. Rolling him onto his back, I don't see the blood, or it doesn't register in my brain until it fills my hands.

I stare down into my best friend's lifeless face.

His eyes are closed, his mouth agape, and the only sound I hear is the blood rushing in my head as I pull him into my lap and curl myself over his body, chanting his name over and over.

*I*t *should have been you.*

The thought comes unbidden, as always, and yet it's no less loud or clear.

At this point it's almost a comfort, like a nagging voice telling me to take out the trash, or put my socks in the hamper. Whatever the annoyance, at least it's with me.

At least it cares.

I open my eyes and stare at the cheap popcorn ceiling in my antiquated hotel room. The days of this memory jarring me awake have long ended. You have to sleep in order to be startled awake. Now, it just plays over and over in my head as I dread the task at hand.

I should have done this eight months ago, after they discharged me from Walter Reed. A bullet to the shoulder and a shredded ACL from when we fell rushed me to Landstuhl for emergency surgery, then back to the U.S. for PT.

Because of that, I missed Staff Sergeant Chad "Jester" Miller's funeral.

It should have been me standing up and telling his family he saved my life.

It should have been me handing the tri-folded flag previously draped over his coffin to his sister, letting her know he was my best friend, as well as my brother in arms.

It should have been me.

Instead, it took me ten months to get my shit together to face her.

Three months in PT.

Another four months in a bottle.

Then three more months of tempered sobriety and

daily workouts to near exhaustion in my parent's basement.

I'm a shit version of my former self, and I know it.

Now I'm lying in a random hotel bed three blocks from his sister's last known address in Spring City, Colorado. I've been here for two days—doing nothing—because I've been too chicken shit to face her or the guys from my old unit.

But today's the day.

I can't put this off any longer.

Today, I find Charity Miller and ask her to forgive me for not being there for her like her brother, my best friend, would have wanted.

Tomorrow, I swing by the Veteran K9 Center to face Karden and Kiki—the man and dog who saved my life.

And then?

I don't know.

Nothing else after that really matters.

There's only a few days left until Christmas, and I made Jester a promise I plan to keep.

VETERAN
K9
TEAM
REPORTING
FOR DUTY

Chapter 1
Bishop

I walk into the lobby of an upscale apartment building near downtown. The floor is marble—or at least it shines like it is—and all the fixtures are glass or chrome. There's a concierge who looks up from his phone, but doesn't ask me where I'm going or if I need help. A bank of windows sits to the East for the morning sunlight, and across the lobby there's another wall of glass showcasing a fountain's rippling reflections of evening sunsets in the West.

The mountains are the perfect backdrop in the distance.

I have to admit it's a beautiful building, but a little posh for a grunt like me.

"Ex-grunt," I remind myself because I'm not sure what I am now.

A washed-up twenty-five-year-old with no job prospects, skills, education, or ambition. Not that it matters to the task at hand. I'm here to keep a promise to my best friend, and then perhaps I'll be able to sleep at night.

Across the foyer, I stop in front of a bank of elevators, just a few steps behind a luscious brunette with the most perfect heart-shaped ass I've ever seen. She's wearing yoga pants, and I mutter thanks to the gods for spandex. I know it sounds cliché, but honestly, is there any greater man-made invention than Lycra?

Her ass is pure perfection. A combination of good genes and a weekly routine of squats and lunges makes her look solid, but soft.

Firm yet squeezable, like she was made to be gripped and kneaded by strong fingers.

Blood rushes south below my belt, and I guess I have another reason to thank the gods today. I was worried I'd never meet a woman in the flesh who caused my mind and body to get in sync again.

I knew I could still get a boner. It was one of the first things I checked when I woke up in the hospital ten months ago. But visibly finding a woman attractive and then having a physical response as I should for a twenty-five-year-old male—this hasn't happened in a long time.

The brunette glances over her shoulder before I can turn away and catches me checking her out.

I nod my head—a scarlet flush hitting my cheeks—and glance up at the numbers above the elevator, trying out a sweet smile that hopefully belies all the dirty thoughts running through my head.

I doubt she's fooled.

The elevator doors open and she steps in. I follow, only then noticing that a key card is required to operate the mechanical beast. She touches her card to the sensor and presses the fifteenth floor, which, coincidentally, is the floor I need.

She glances over her shoulder. "Which floor?"

"I'm also going to the fifteenth floor."

She raises an eyebrow, but turns and faces forward as if to ignore me. Too bad. I like the way she looks. Her eyes, big and brown, are a little too large for her face, yet beautiful like a skittish doe. She has high cheekbones and plump, kissable lips that I'm sure have driven many men's fantasies into territories well beyond kissing.

Definitely made for sucking.

The ends of her long, straight, chestnut locks brush against her lower back, drawing my eyes back down to her ass.

I lean against the corner of the elevator and fold my arms across my chest as the elevator doors close and the car moves, closing my eyes briefly before she catches me checking her out again.

Taking a deep breath, I let it out slowly. Fuck me, I hate tight spaces, although this elevator isn't that small. I mean, I could lie down on my back and let her ride me, so that means the elevator is at least six and a half feet wide.

Jesus Christ, Bishop! Get your mind out of the gutter. This poor girl is just trying to get home in peace.

These are the thoughts I will myself to have—I try to

be a good guy, after all—and yet, as soon as I open my eyes, my gaze is drawn back down to her ass.

Really, I just need to get laid. It's been too long, and as soon as I'm done with this task, it's next on the list of things to do. It's been fourteen months, and even though my therapist says a relationship is the last thing I need right now, I'm thinking sinking in between the thighs of the right woman might chase away some of the bad dreams and finally let me get a good night's sleep.

It's certainly one of the few distractions that I think are healthy for me right now. Healthier than drugs or alcohol, the latter of which I gave up a few months ago once I recognized I was using it as a crutch. The day you realize the only sleep you get is because you're passing out is the day you have to say no.

The elevator stops on the fifth floor, but the doors don't open. She looks up at the display and then punches the button for the fifteenth floor again, but nothing lights up on the panel. Then she uses her key card and pushes the fifteenth floor again, and again nothing lights up.

I hear her mumbling under her breath, "What the hell?"

Attempting to keep my shit calm, I roll my shoulders and ask, "Is this a common problem?"

She shrugs and glances over her shoulder at me again. "Not in the last year that I've lived here."

At this point, I'm not freaking out, but I can feel my anxiety spiking.

Tight space.

No clear escape.

Shit.

And then the lights go out.

We're plunged into darkness for a few seconds before emergency lighting illuminates the small space in a greenish pallor.

"Dammit. It had to be green," I mutter to myself, but apparently loud enough for her to hear. She glances over her shoulder again, her brow raised. A fine sheen of sweat breaks out on my forehead, and the feeling of weightlessness creeps up on me fast. I'm trying to hold it together, folding my arms tighter across my chest, but it's no use and I sag against the wall until my ass hits the floor.

"Are you okay?" She's kneeling beside me, and while I see her and know she's next to me, her voice sounds like she's speaking from the other end of a tunnel.

I nod, but the ability to form words escapes me.

"Are you having an anxiety attack?" She reaches out to touch me but then pulls her hand back, like she knows I'm not really here right now and there's no telling what I'm capable of doing.

Honestly, I'm not sure what I'm capable of.

Swallowing the lump in my throat, I nod. "I'll be okay. I just need a few minutes."

"What can I do for you?"

"Do you have a weighted blanket on you?" I try to joke, but I can't seem to chuckle with any kind of humor.

She frowns. "No. Does that help?"

I nod again. "I feel like I'm floating, and the blanket grounds me."

Biting her lip, she puts her bag down. "What if I hugged you? Do you think that would work?"

Without answering, I pull her onto my lap and crush her against my chest, my arms wrapping tightly around her lush body. I close my eyes, blocking out the green that reminds me of night vision goggles and midnight maneuvers. Sweet orange candy takes root in my mind, and I realize I'm smelling it on her. Is it her hair or does she have candy in her mouth? I don't know, but I'm grasping on to the question like a lifeline, as it gives my brain something new to focus on.

I'm not sure how much time passes as I sit here focusing on taking slow, steady breaths, but I'm feeling better.

She attempts to shift in my lap and pats my bicep, which is locked in a death grip around her. I relax my arms and open my eyes, but I don't look around, and I try hard to not focus on the fact that she's cast in the horrific green hue of my nightmares. Instead, I focus on her doll-like eyes, cute button nose, and perfectly pouty lips. She's beautiful, and while it might be wrong, given our current situation, I find focusing on my attraction is better than thinking about our predicament.

"Sorry. I didn't mean to manhandle you like that."

She smiles. "It's okay. Are you feeling better?"

I nod. "Thanks to you."

Shifting her ass, I think she's getting ready to stand up and reflexively I tighten my grip. "Don't get up."

"I wasn't going to get up, but I think I'm crushing you."

"You're not. If you're uncomfortable, we can adjust, but please don't leave. Not yet."

"I'm your human weighted blanket for as long as you need, but I need to adjust."

I release my death grip on her. She shifts her ass, so she's sitting on the ground between my legs. Although I hadn't noticed, it alleviates the pressure on my dick. Then she leans her body against mine and nuzzles her face into my neck, her arms wrapped around my waist. I loop my arms around her, concentrating on keeping them loose, and we drop into a comfortable silence. I breathe her in—my sweet citrus angel—and thank the gods for giving her to me during this whatever-the-fuck is going on moment with the elevator.

"Hello? Are you okay down there?" A male voice from beyond calls out to us.

She lifts her head and speaks toward the ceiling. "Yeah, we're okay. What's going on?"

"Seems to be an electrical problem, ma'am. We believe the back current smoked the computer board controlling the brain of this elevator, so it's confused about where it is and where it's going. Part of the safety mechanism is to shut down when that happens and lock the car in place. You are currently between the fifth and sixth floor. We have an engineer heading our way. Her ETA is twenty minutes, but if someone is hurt, we also have the fire department ready to pull you out."

She looks at me, her eyebrow cocked in a high arch. "What do you think? Can you chill with me for another twenty minutes, or do you want the fire department to shimmy down the cables and pull us out?"

"I can chill with you if you're willing to stay on as my security blanket." I lean my head back and close my eyes again, soaking in the comfort her body provides me.

"We're okay to wait on the engineer."

"Yes ma'am. We're stationed on the sixth floor. If you need us, just yell up. We'll send someone down."

She tucks her head under my chin and resumes her position, snuggled up against my chest. If she's uncomfortable with this, she doesn't show it. "Which do you prefer? Silence or talking?"

"I'm not much of a talker, but I like the sound of your voice. It's soothing. If you're willing, I'd like to sit here and listen to you for a bit."

"Wow. A man asking a woman to ramble on? Is this the end of days or what?"

I chuckle, because she's probably right. "I don't mind having a woman talk to me, even when she's rambling. My mom's a rambler."

"Okay. Well, then I'll give you a choice. One—I can tell you about a typically boring day in my life. Two—I can tell you about the last movie I saw. Spoiler alert, it was a horror movie and the girl in platform heels totally gives it up to her boyfriend, but they die before either of them gets off. Or three—I can tell you about the book I'm reading right now, but I have to warn you, it is a steamy romance novel."

Opening my eyes, I shake my head, unsure I heard her correctly. I can't see her face, because she's got her head tucked under my chin, but I can feel her smiling against my throat. "Let me make sure I heard you correctly. I have a beautiful woman sitting in my lap offering to tell me a dirty story?"

She giggles and shrugs. "It's an option."

"And it's the one I'm going to take."

VETERAN
K9
TEAM
REPORTING
FOR DUTY

Chapter 2
Charity

I don't know what possesses me to tell a stranger a story about attraction, love, and sex—lots of sex—but for the next fifteen minutes I regale him with a tale about a couple who coincidentally met in a broken down elevator. I thought it was fitting, given the situation. Of course, they were submerged in darkness while we can see each other—albeit, I'm not looking at his face.

I'm not making any eye contact, because if I were, I'd never be able to recite it.

Although, I don't have to see his face to know my story has had its intended effect. Instead of spiraling down some anxiety rabbit hole, he's focused on me, in the present and now. And because I have my cheek resting against his chest, I notice when his breathing changes and his heartbeat races in tune with the story.

He's turned on by the romance, albeit mildly, but he's also a gentleman. He hasn't used the sexy story or the fact that I'm sitting in his lap to make a move. His hands have stayed clasped around my back, and he hasn't shifted me to where I'm sitting on his cock again, which I haven't checked on since I started telling him about the book.

If he's hard, I don't want to know.

Well, I kind of do want to know, because he's hot, and when I caught him checking out my ass earlier, it took everything within me not to shimmy my hips. I should be above flaunting my curves to gain a guy's attention, but considering I never get the time of day from most men, having this hottie notice and appreciate my well-worked-out booty is a significant boost to my ego.

Sue me. I'm a feminist, but that doesn't mean I don't enjoy the right man's attention when it's on my terms.

At the end of my story, I'm met with silence, which is less than comforting. My brother didn't call me Chatty Charity for nothing. "How are you feeling?"

"Thoroughly distracted. Thank you." He chuckles, and this time it's genuine versus the forced guffaw he attempted earlier.

"I haven't seen you in the building before. Did you just move in?" I wonder, because the fifteenth floor only has ten units, and although I don't know everyone on my floor, I would have remembered seeing him.

"No. I'm dropping in on a friend."

"Oh." I wonder if it is a woman and search my memories for a single supermodel on my floor that would be worthy of a man like him. He's sexy—tall and blonde with blue eyes and a square jaw—and considering I've been pressed against his body for the better part of the last half-hour, he's built like a Greek god. All hard, chiseled muscle and no fat, which isn't necessarily my type of guy.

I myself have a bit of a cushion, even more so after the last year. Stress coupled with depression does that to a person—me specifically. I cope by indulging in whatever makes me happy, and unlike people who turn to drugs or alcohol, my drug of choice is sugar, which I've read is more addictive than cocaine. I'm not sure if that's true, but the diet salespeople purport that rumor, and I kind of believe it.

My brother would have told me to lay off the dingdongs, meaning the tasty snack cakes as well as the horrible men I date, because he thought he was funny.

I guess he was pretty funny.

I miss him so much.

This guy reminds me of Chad, and I'm wondering if his comment about the green light coupled with his anxiety attack means he served in the military?

Like in the movies when they do combat maneuvers at night and everything has the green tint to it. I mean, why else would the emergency lighting freak you out?

"Can I ask you a question?" I hedge, because I don't want to upset him again. He seems to be completely chill at the moment, and while his skin is warm, he's no longer sweating.

"Sure."

"Are you in the Army?"

He stiffens for a second and drags in a ragged breath before relaxing. "It's the hair, isn't it? I thought growing it out would take the military veneer off of me."

I chuckle. "No, it's not that. You kind of remind me of my brother." I lift my head slightly, and my nose scrapes along his stubbled jaw. He smells good—musky, with a hint of sandalwood, which I bet is from his body wash and not cologne.

He doesn't strike me as the cologne type.

He tilts his head down, his brow furrowed, and opens his dark blue eyes. "Is your brother military?"

A sad smile creeps on my face as I envision Chad's derpy smile, the one he reserved specifically for me as his little sister. "He was. He was killed in combat earlier this year."

The look on my stranger's face sucks all the air out of the tiny space, and the bottom of my stomach plummets as I get a dreadful feeling.

"Are you Charity?"

I pull back from his chest and bring my hands to my lap, tears instantly filling my eyes. His arms fall to his sides, but his gaze searches my face, as if he's putting together a puzzle and I'm the missing piece.

"Who are you?" I ask in the way of an answer.

He blows out a breath, but doesn't take his eyes off me. "I'm Bishop. Your brother was my best friend. I'm here for you."

"What?" I scrunch up my face, trying to keep the tears from falling. After Chad died, I got a visit from some nameless soldier who brought me the news. Honestly, Chad's military unit was great. As his only living relative, they offered me all kinds of support, but at the time, I wasn't interested. I wanted nothing to do with the military, considering they took the last of my blood from me. Even though they buried Chad in Arlington, I held a small service where a few classmates, some aunts and uncles, and a few distant cousins dropped by. Since our parents died several years ago, it had really only been me and Chad—the dynamic duo—left in Colorado. I never replied to any of his unit's inquiries, and after a month or two of ignoring them, they went radio silent.

Bishop swallows hard and then clears his throat. "We were deployed together, and he'd asked me to check in on you if he didn't make it home."

"You were with him?" I can't stop the tears from rolling down my face when I see tears well up in his own eyes.

"I was." The way he says those words—his tone filled with hollowed pain—I realize he wasn't just overseas with my brother, he was right there, probably by my brother's side as he took his final breath. I can't stop myself from bawling—ten months of pent-up emotions spewing out of me all at once—and I throw myself against his chest. He wraps his arms around me and holds me tight, his cheek resting on the top of my head.

I cry for several minutes. Long enough that my head hurts, my nose is running, and I've drenched Bishop's T-shirt.

He holds me tight, lets me cry, and doesn't say a word.

"Is everything okay down there?" the voice from above calls down to us.

Sniffling, I try to pull myself together and pull back from Bishop's chest.

"How much longer?" I call into the void, my voice cracking in the darkness.

"The engineer is swapping out the board now. We should have you moving in the next five to ten minutes. Are you sure you're okay, ma'am?"

He either hears me crying or notes the shakiness in my voice. I force a smile, hoping it will change my tone. "We're fine, but ready to get off this ride."

"Yes, ma'am. We sincerely apologize and will get you out of there shortly."

I nod, not that the voice above can see me. I lock gazes with Bishop, who tentatively brings his hand to my face. With a gentle swipe of his thumb, he wipes at the tears and cups my cheeks. "I'm sorry we had to meet like this."

"In an elevator or because Chad asked you to come?" I smile, but it doesn't reach my eyes.

He gives me a similar smile. "Both."

"You know..." I search his face, a war of emotions—sadness, anger, confusion, exhaustion—battling in my chest. Who is this guy, and why would my brother send a stranger to me? "Chad never mentioned a Bishop. Actually, he talked about none of the guys he deployed with."

He shakes his head. "Yeah, he was very protective of you. And considering a lot of the guys got off on giving each other shit about their hot girlfriends or hotter sisters back home, Miller barely talked about you. He didn't want any of the guys getting any bright ideas or giving him shit about you, so I'm not surprised he didn't tell you about us, either."

"And yet, he sent you to me."

The muscles in his jaw flex. "He trusted me. The plan had been for me to come home for Christmas with him this year. So here I am—if you'll have me."

The lights inside the elevator turn on seconds before the elevator moves. I scramble off Bishop's lap and jump to my feet. He's a lot slower standing up, but is on his feet when the elevator doors open on the sixth floor. Two paramedics are standing by with the apartment complex manager.

"Thank god, you're okay." The manager exhales dramatically.

"I told you we were fine."

"Do either of you require medical attention?" One paramedic asks as her gaze slides over Bishop in a salacious manner. His T-shirt is crumbled and there's a wet spot from my tears on his right pec.

Probably some snot, too—so that's sexy.

Even a mess he is drool-worthy, so I get the gleam in her eye. She glances at me and gives me a knowing smile.

Oh, I wish that was why he was rumpled.

"I'm good. You?" I glance at Bishop, but his gaze is on the floor with his hands stuffed into the pockets of his jeans.

"No medical attention required, but thank you for standing by," he says.

"That's our job." The other paramedic grumbles and picks up his bag.

"Are you ready to head up?" I turn to Bishop. I don't know this man, but at this point I feel closer to him than I've felt to anyone other than my brother. He came for me, came for my brother, probably because Chad didn't want me to spend my first Christmas without him alone.

He glances up, meets my eye, and then nods. "Let's go."

VETERAN
K9
TEAM
REPORTING
FOR DUTY

Chapter 3
Bishop

Great first impression, bud.

First, I get busted checking out the ass of my best friend's sister, which is exactly why he kept me away from her in the first place. Then, I have a complete meltdown and wrap her in a stranglehold—my personal lifeline—when the whole reason I'm here is to be her lifeline as we get through her first Christmas without Miller.

"Stairs or elevator?" She gives me a small, knowing smile.

"Stairs, if you don't mind. I need to work off some of this nervous energy."

"Okay, but it's nine flights, so no judgment if I'm sweating and wheezing by the time we get there."

"Are you asthmatic?" While I could avoid an elevator for the rest of my life, I don't want to cause a medical emergency. I mean, we got this far without needing the paramedics, and there's no reason to test fate.

She shakes her head. "No. I'm just out of shape."

"You look perfect to me." I mutter and turn to the hall to look for the stairwell. I didn't mean it as a come-on, but I'm betting that's how it sounds because as soon as I said it, I'm reminded of just how perfect she is. Miller was right to never have shown me a picture of her. I would have spent the last year fantasizing about her, anxious about the day we met.

We find the stairwell and ascend the first flight in silence. We're taking it slow, and I'm betting it is because she's as emotionally drained and physically exhausted as I am.

"So," she prompts. "You had planned to spend Christmas with me and Chad? Don't you have a family to spend the holidays with?"

"I do, but they know this is important to me." I grab onto the handrail as my knee aches. Mostly, it doesn't bother me. Months of physical therapy have done their job and then some, but I typically avoid the stairs, as well as lunges and squats.

Slow and steady, we go.

"I appreciate you being here. I mean, you promised Chad, and it's sweet that you followed through on your promise, but I'm fine. You don't have to babysit me through the holidays."

I grab her arm and pull her to a stop on the landing between the ninth and tenth floors. "Yes, I made your brother a promise, but I also wanted to come. I've been looking forward to meeting you since last Christmas, when he bitched about being in the field while you were alone."

She frowned. "Last Christmas was great. He sent me to the Bahamas."

"Yeah, and it pained him not to be there, too. That's the first time he really told me about you, and we made plans to do something bigger and better this year." I scowl at the ground. "I'm sorry I didn't plan something bigger, and I'm sorry I didn't get here sooner. It took me a long time to get my shit together."

She places her hand on my face, and I bring my eyes up to meet hers. "I'm glad you're here. No apologies are necessary."

Damn, I could get lost in her big, dark eyes. They are like endless pools on a midnight swim, tempting and inviting.

I clear my throat and take a step back. Chuckling, I turn and take the next flight of steps, even slower than before. "Damn. Miller was right to not let any of us near you."

"What's that supposed to mean?"

"You already busted me checking you out. He'd have killed me if I'd done that in front of him."

She laughs. "Yeah, you'd be a spot on the wall."

"And, well—" I can't seem to stop my mouth from spilling all my secrets "—I had every intention of asking you out once we were rescued."

"You did?" Her voice raises an octave and I'm surprised that she's surprised. Could she not tell how attracted I was to her? I mean, before we figured out our connection.

Who am I kidding? I'm still attracted to her, even

more now because I know a lot about her. The only detail Miller left out was how, physically, she's exactly my type: dark hair, dark eyes, and curvy.

Of course, he left out that tidbit.

I would have too if I had a sister I was keeping my horn-dog buddies away from. But I also know the basics. She's kind, smart, sometimes goofy, and good with children. She works as a classroom assistant, specifically with autistic kids, which explains how she handled me so well in the elevator. I've been told anxiety attacks and over-stimulation are similar, so some of the same coping mech-anisms work for both. That's how I got the weighted blanket idea from my therapist three months ago after I gave up the liquor and the pain pills.

Before Miller died, I'd been looking forward to this Christmas, to meeting Charity and having a fun-filled week wherever we ended up. But now that I've seen her and have held her in my arms, I'm thinking that week would have been a special kind of hell, too, because there is no way I wouldn't have been attracted to her, and no way Miller wouldn't have picked up on and crushed me for it.

Of course, now everything is different.

I'm different, and I'm sure she is, too.

"Well, I guess my brother was right not to tell me about you, too." Her gaze is on the steps in front of us. "If you had asked me out, I would've said yes."

I did not need to know that.

Fantasies of what-if will make me crazy over the next few days with that piece of information. I wasn't sure how this interaction was going to go today. Even though I suspected awkwardness, tears, and at least one day of bone-weary emotions, I hadn't expected to feel an intense draw toward her, too. I've never had a fierce wave of calm come over me like what happened with her in the elevator today. Nothing and no one has ever grounded me so quickly, making me feel whole versus splintering apart and floating up into the ether. It's not only about how fucking gorgeous she is, but she soothes me like nothing else, and that includes alcohol or adrenaline.

We pass the fourteenth floor and my heart is beating fast in my chest, and it isn't the exertion of the climb causing the ticker to thump. I'm going to do something crazy, something Miller would not have approved of, but I've never been more sure of anything in my life. "Would you have dinner with me tonight?"

She side-eyes me, her cheeks flush as a thin bead of sweat rolls down the back of her neck. "Are you asking me out?"

"Yeah, I am."

We get to the fifteenth floor and she motions to the left. At her door, she touches the key card to her door handle, and it clicks open. "Welcome to my home."

I follow her inside, greeted by a bank of windows facing the park. The room is tastefully decorated, if not sparse, and she has all of her furniture arranged so her view is the world that lies beyond.

"Wow," I breathe, standing in front of the windows. The building curves in an arc facing the city, but Charity chose an apartment that faces away from the skyline, affording her miles of gorgeous green tree tops and mountains in the distance. There are no other apartments with a view into her windows, and my mind goes to a place it shouldn't.

But damn, how hot would it be to take her against these windows?

"So, dinner?" I turn at her reflection in the windows, not missing the fact she hasn't accepted my invitation.

She nods. "We can go to dinner. Where are you staying?"

"I'm in a hotel a few blocks from here."

"Oh." She bites her lip and hands me a glass of water.

I glance around her apartment, which encompasses the living room, kitchen, and dining table. It's a large open floor plan, and roomy with her few furnishings, which helps me breathe easier after our elevator experience. Against one wall are bookshelves stuffed with books that are arranged by cover color, creating an interesting rainbow effect. Picture frames and knick-knacks sit in front of and between stacks of books. I check them out, soaking in photos of her parents and friends, but I'm drawn to one of her and Miller at her college graduation. He was proud of her, and once he opened up to me, would tell me about what was going on in her life back home whenever he got updates. For instance, I knew he hated the guys she dated. He referred to them as ass-clowns, which, coincidently, is one of my go-to insults.

"About dinner tonight..." Charity says softly. "Are you asking me as Chad's sister, or as the woman whose butt you were admiring before we got on the elevator?"

I raise my brow, impressed she faced that head on and called me out on it. "I feel like there are implications tied to whichever answer I give you."

"Well, my brother and his friend would've crashed in my guest room for Christmas, but the guy checking out my ass an hour ago wouldn't."

"I guess I'm not sleeping in your guest room."

She takes a drink of her water, hiding her smile behind the glass. "Okay then."

VETERAN
K9
TEAM
REPORTING
FOR DUTY

Chapter 4
Charity

Bishop has a bag of stuff to give me back at his hotel and said he'd bring it when he took me to dinner tonight. Knowing he'll have Chad's stuff with him, I suggest we eat in, as I do not want to get emotional in public. Then I asked for a few hours to shower, shop, and get ready.

That was three hours ago. I'm emotionally wrecked after our elevator experience, and then another thorough cry in the tub. It's been a while since I let myself fall apart, and while I've been actively avoiding Christmas cheer—I don't have a single holiday decoration in my apartment—I've been holding it together by avoiding the radio and TV for the last month. That means no Christmas music, no movies, no old favorite holiday sitcom episodes to remind me of Chad.

I know Christmas Day is going to be rough, but now that Bishop is here, it might not be that bad.

So I did what I often do... I took a hot bath and talked

to my brother, asking him what I should do. But this conversation was different, because this time I asked him why.

Why did he send Bishop to me?

What had been his plan if he'd come home, too?

Had he caused that freak accident in the elevator to give us a chance to push past all the awkwardness that would've come if Bishop had shown up at my door, unannounced, as planned?

Please don't think I'm crazy, but I believe he did. I believe Chad had every intention of bringing Bishop and me together, whether or not he was alive. There is something about Bishop. I felt it the moment I caught him checking me out, but more so when he held me, like I was the only thing tethering him to this world. I don't want to take advantage of him in a vulnerable state, so I'll never admit it to him, but I felt a connection between us, as if we were meant to be together.

I climb out of my bath feeling a lot better about everything, and I'm excited to share an evening with the one piece of Chad that wasn't already mine. I gave Bishop my extra key card so he could bypass the garage and elevator security, but am pleased when he knocks on my door instead of letting himself in.

Opening the door, I blush when he hands me a bouquet of red roses and white carnations with tiny pinecones and sprigs of juniper. "These are beautiful. You didn't have to—"

"Yeah, I did." He follows me inside and sets down a small duffle bag. "I came here to take care of you, and instead you took care of me in the elevator. I'll never be able to thank you enough."

"You took care of me, too, judging by the wet stain I left on your T-shirt."

He smiles, and it makes me all tingly inside. "What smells good?"

"Ah." I hold up a finger and walk into the kitchen. "I made spaghetti, garlic bread, and green salad. I also have wine. Do you prefer red or white?"

Shaking his head, he waves away the wine. "None for me. I'll be fine with water."

"You don't drink wine?"

"I don't drink, period. I gave it up a few months ago when it became a coping mechanism."

"Oh, okay." I put the wine down, impressed by his self-awareness and control. "Would you like ice in your water?"

"That would be great."

I point to where we'll be sitting and hand him two ice waters. "Sit down and I'll get you a plate. Any food no-nos I need to know about?"

"Nope. I'm a trash compactor and will eat whatever you put in front of me."

"Just like Chad." I chuckle and then wince, wondering if talking about my brother will bring me more pitying looks. Honestly, that's been the hardest part about all of this. I've had no one to talk to because everyone gets weird when I talk about my dead brother.

I glance over at Bishop, who has a goofy grin on his face.

"Did he ever tell you about the time we got a care package full of Korean snack foods?"

"No." I plate up our dinners and sit across from him.

"Some of it was good, but then there was some weird shit in there, too. Like salted, dehydrated squid chips."

"Ewww." I scrunch up my nose.

Bishop laughs. "Yeah, we challenged each other to consume every bite. It wasn't as bad as you'd think."

For the next two hours, Bishop shares stories from the last two years of training and deployments, all of which have me laughing until tears roll down my cheeks.

"I always knew Chad was a prankster, but I didn't know he was the unit jester." I laugh and tuck my feet up underneath me. We've moved from the table and are now sitting on the couch. Bishop pulls out his phone, thumbing through photos and sharing them with me. I see a whole new side of Chad, one he kept hidden whenever he came home. He always shielded me from his military duties, and I never understood why. I was proud of him, and I knew he loved his job.

"Actually, he and I competed for that title. We were always trying to one-up each other, and our unit knew they were in for it when we teamed up. No one was safe. I mean, no one."

I scoot toward him so I can see the photos better. To my delight, Bishop throws his arm around me and pulls me even closer. He smells good, and the warmth from his body infuses me with endorphins. All I want to do is crawl into his lap and nuzzle his neck like I did this afternoon, sans the tears, bathing in the feel-good vibes emanating from his soul.

He stops swiping across the photos and pauses on one of him and Chad in full combat gear. They have their arms crossed over their chests, and they're leaning against each other in a bro stance, grinning at the camera.

"That's an amazing picture."

Bishop lets out a big breath. "It's the last one we took before..." He lets the words hang out there, but we both know what he means.

I use my fingers and enlarge the photo, zeroing in on their helmet and chin-strapped faces. "He looks happy. You both do."

"I miss him." Bishop drops his phone into his lap.

I turn to face him, finding his eyes on me. "I miss him, too."

His gaze drops to my lips before coming back to my eyes. "I'm sorry it took me so long to come to you."

"You were there when he died." I stare versus ask, because deep down, I already know the truth. I can see the pain in Bishop's eyes, and can only imagine the horrors he's seen. It's oddly satisfying to soothe the person who has come to take care of me. There's a connection between us that goes beyond our love for my brother. I feel like Bishop recognizes and accepts the broken pieces of me, just as I recognize and accept the broken pieces of him. No one has talked to me plainly about losing my brother. They always tiptoe around the topic or give me the uncomfortable, pitying press of their lips as they struggle to find words.

I get it. They don't know what to say to make me feel better because there is nothing for them to say. Nothing is going to bring Chad back, although Bishop is giving me something no one else can give me—the pieces of my brother I never had.

He nods. "Miller saved my life. I took a bullet in the shoulder, but if he hadn't thrown me to the ground, I wouldn't be here today."

Pressing my palm to his cheek, I give him a weak smile. "I know my brother, and he doesn't regret saving your life one bit."

He swallows a lump in his throat. "It should have been me."

"Don't say that." I shake my head vehemently. "Never say that."

Bishop sighs. "It's just, he had you to come home to—someone who actually depended upon him to make it back. You lost the last member of your family, and it's not fair."

We stare at each other for a minute, saying nothing. Then I go for broke. "Can I tell you something without you thinking I'm crazy?"

"Of course." The furrow between his eyebrows deepens.

"I talk to Chad all the time. When I'm sad, or confused, or simply frustrated with work. Even when I'm happy or bored."

"Does he talk back?"

I nod. "In his own way."

Bishop smiles. "Can I tell you something without you

thinking I'm crazy?"

I giggle. "Yes."

"I think he broke the elevator today."

Gasping, my mouth hangs open. "Me, too."

"It was such a Miller move." He shakes his head, his eyes bouncing to the windows before coming back to me. "I was nervous about coming here. In the last couple months, I've drafted you over a dozen emails, called and hung up several times, so it seems fitting that once I stepped inside the building, he took over and threw us into a crisis that I couldn't avoid."

"That sounds like our Chad." I drop my hand from his cheek and rest it over his heart.

Bishop's body is tight, coiled, as he stares back at me. His breathing changes, as if he's trying to control his erratic heartbeat under my palm. "Thank you for not turning me away this afternoon."

I lick my lips, and his gaze drops again. Heat blooms in my chest as anticipation builds in my belly. "Thank you for coming to see me."

He swallows again, his gaze bouncing between my eyes and my lips, and I think I might die if he doesn't make a move.

"Bishop?"

"Yes, Charity?"

"Are you thinking about kissing me?"

"Yeah, I am."

I don't wait for him to make a move. I push my mouth against his, no longer able to handle the anticipation. Bishop brings his hand into my hair and cradles my neck as he turns his head and deepens the kiss. He licks at my lips and I part them willingly, moaning as his tongue darts in and dances with mine. I'm not sure if I push, or he pulls, but within seconds I'm in his lap, and he's wrapping his arms around me to hold me close.

Bishop alternates between tender and loving, to hard and passionate, as if he's questioning whether this is right or wrong. I understand because part of me is desperate for him. I've been looking for someone like him—someone I am attracted to that instantly makes me feel comfortable and safe—my entire life, and to date, I've failed epically.

But he was also Chad's best friend—the last guy to see my brother alive—which will always hang over our heads. Even if I treasure the reminder, maybe he doesn't want Chad's death weighing on him for the rest of his life.

I push off his chest and break our kiss. His hands have traveled up and down my back, tangled in my hair, and tentatively ran down my hips, yet I notice he's avoided my ass, and his fingers have come nowhere near my inner thighs or aching clit screaming for his touch.

I mean, this man can kiss, so I'm ready, but the more inside his head he is, the more inside my head I get, and soon neither of us will enjoy this.

"Are you okay?" I ask, searching his face for the truth of what he wants. Does he really want me, or is this a night of emotion that we will both regret in the morning?

Any other guy, and I'd say he wants me. Badly.

"Yes, but I don't want to take advantage of the situation. It's been an emotional day, and I don't want you to do something you'll regret."

"Are you afraid you'll regret it?"

His gaze travels down my body, lingering long enough for me to know he wants to touch me. "No."

I grab his hands, which he's resting on the outsides of my mid-thighs, and bring them to my breasts. He sucks in his breath, instinctively kneading my flesh through my top, his thumb swiping over my nipples until they are taut and aching for his mouth.

I moan and throw my head back, grinding my pussy down on his cock.

"Fuck, Charity." His touch turns hungry, his fingers more insistent.

Shaking my head, I bring my gaze back to his. "I'm not going to regret anything, Bishop. I want this. I want you."

He lets go of my breasts and slides one hand into my hair, wrapping his other arm around my waist. And then I'm on my back, looking up at him as he looms over me with the hottest and hungriest look in his eyes. He runs his hands reverently over my breasts before tugging up my shirt. I lift and he pulls it off, discarding it over the back of the couch. "It's been a while for me, so I may not last long the first time."

"We'll be doing it more than once?" I grin up at him teasingly.

He grins back at me. "I'm thinking all night and into the morning, if you'll have me."

"I'll have you."

VETERAN
K9
TEAM
REPORTING
FOR DUTY

Chapter 5
Bishop

Before I came back to Charity's apartment, I'd done some quick soul searching, asking if my attraction to her was a betrayal to Miller. I mean, they were brother and sister, not man and wife, so ultimately I decided that if my intentions are good, this is not a betrayal. I can't help it if she's perfect for me, and I wonder if Miller knew that all along. It's not like he ever told any of the other guys about his sister, nor had he planned to introduce any of them to her.

I walked into her apartment intending to make her mine, but not in some chest-thumping, caveman kind of way. With the emotional turmoil bringing us together, I'm willing to take my time because I want her to believe we are meant to be.

So, when she kisses me, I'm unsure how to react. What I want to do is roll her to her back, pin her down, and explore every inch of her delectable curves until there is no fraction of her body that hasn't felt my hands or tongue.

But I don't want to scare her off either.

How lucky am I that she's a woman who knows what she wants?

Charity's lush curves are mine for the taking, and the lacy pink bra she has on barely contains her full breasts. I push them together and run my tongue along her cleavage before I pull the fabric down and latch on to her nipple with my teeth. She moans and arches up, her fingers digging into my scalp as I alternate between her breasts. Charity responds perfectly, ramping up my desire and desperation to strip off her clothing.

She grabs my shirt, and I let go of her long enough to pull it off and toss it across the room. She giggles at my enthusiasm, and while I'm glad she's comfortable, what I really want to hear is her screaming my name. I stand up long enough to pop the buttons on my jeans and wiggle my hips to make them fall to the floor. At the same time, I'm peeling her yoga pants off her long, lush legs. The tiniest strip of pale pink fabric covers her below, and my mouth waters at the feast she's planned for me.

"Do you always wear matching bras and panties?" I want to know if this is the norm or if she did it for me.

I really hope she did it for me.

"Not always." She blushes and bites her lip.

"Did you do it for me?"

"I did it for you," she admits.

I tenderly drop between her legs, careful of my

damaged knee. "Spread your legs for me, baby, so I can thank you properly."

She spreads her thighs for me, and I move the thin wisp of fabric aside, diving in face first, my tongue lapping at her with no finesse, no preamble. I want to smother myself in her pussy, eating her with the vigor a starved man like me has to give.

"Oh, god!" she cries out, arching her hips off the couch. I lift her thigh with my shoulder and spread her wider, while I use my other arm to pin down her waist, testing out the sensitivity of her clit by tonguing and then sucking until she's bucking against my mouth. I resist plunging my fingers inside of her, intent on getting her off this first time with only my mouth. Later, I'll find out how sensitive her g-spot is, and then, even later, I'll figure out which combination gets her off the fastest and the hardest. I plan on having a lifetime to learn these things about her, and yet, I'm like a kid who has to know everything there is to know right now.

"Bishop, I'm going to come." She's got her fingers in my hair, and she's fisting my longer locks at the same time she's pressing my face against her sweet pussy.

I say nothing and suck her clit harder until she's breaking apart and screaming my name—exactly like I want. She's shaking against my mouth as I let go of her clit, and I give her a few seconds—waiting until her death grip in my hair relaxes—before I bring my face up to look at her. Her eyes are closed, mouth is open, and she's panting in the most glorious way that makes her breasts rise and fall in a mesmerizing rhythm.

Shucking off my boxers, I climb up her body, trailing kisses along the way until I'm hovering over her face. She pulls me into a scorching kiss and shifts her hips so I'm seated perfectly between her thighs, my hard and aching cock weeping with a need to thrust fast and deep inside of her.

"How do you feel?" I ask her between kisses.

"Amazing." She sighs as she wraps one leg around the small of my back and pulls my hips closer. I guess the yoga pants aren't just a fashion statement as my girl demonstrates her flexibility and her need to have me fill her like only I can.

I push into her slowly, sucking in my breath at how tight she fits around my cock. Maybe I should have primed her with my fingers because she's deliciously tight and my confidence of lasting a few minutes is waning. I'll be lucky if I last a few seconds when she feels this good.

She gasps as I push my hips forward, fully seating myself inside her hot, wet pussy. I groan and push my face into the crook of her neck, concentrating on holding back the orgasm I haven't rocked in weeks. Once I feel in control, I move my hips slow and steady as her body clenches around me, milking me for the release I'm fighting to hold back.

"Dammit, you feel good. So fucking tight," I breathe against her neck.

"Bishop, I need you," she moans, her fingers digging into my shoulders.

"You've got me, baby," I say, continuing the unhurried pace, focusing on building her orgasm before I lose control over my own.

"No, I mean I need you. Please. I'm so close."

"What do you want me to do?" I'll do anything she asks to feel her climax around my cock.

"Faster. Harder. Please."

Fuck—there goes lasting a few minutes. I quicken the pace, hitting her as fast and hard as she demands. She throws her head back and screams my name as her pussy clamps tight around my cock... and I'm lost. I can't hold back any longer, and I come hard inside of her, stars filling my vision as my balls tighten and tingle with my release.

I collapse on top of her, and although I'm sure I'm crushing her, I'm physically wiped out as I fight to catch my breath. When my brain re-engages with the rest of my body, I reach down and grab my shirt, using it to clean us up. Without asking if she was on the pill, I came inside of her, claiming her as my own. And honestly, I'm not the least bit upset about it.

Hopefully, she isn't either.

Hopefully, she knows this is it for us.

It's her and I, together—forever.

"You are perfect." I roll off the couch and pull her down on top of me, adjusting until she's straddling me like I want. She still has on her bra and underwear, although I'm thinking I shredded her panties when I pulled them aside with too much enthusiasm.

Fuck it. I'll buy her new ones.

She smiles down at me. "You're fairly perfect yourself."

"You know this isn't a one-night thing for me, right? I'm here for as long as you'll have me."

Placing her hand over my heart, she leans down and plants a sweet kiss on my lips. "I know. Chad wouldn't have sent you to me if this wasn't something real for both of us."

"You believe he sent me to you?"

She blushes. "I do."

"And here I thought he was acting as my guardian angel and sent you to me."

"Maybe he sent us to each other."

"That sounds right. Tricky little fucker was always watching out for me." I slide my hands into her hair and pull her down for another kiss. "Where do you want to go for Christmas?"

"What do you mean?" She lies on top of me and nestles her face into my neck. Her hair smells like oranges, so I figure it's got to be her shampoo, and her warm breath on my skin causes blood to run straight to my dick, which is gearing up for round two.

I trail my fingers over her lush body. "Well... originally, Miller thought the three of us would go to Hawaii or Cancun or something like that. If I'd been here months ago like I was supposed to be, maybe we could have pulled off planning something like that. As it is, I have a truck, a full tank of gas, and nothing but time, so if I can get us there, I will. You just have to tell me where you want to go."

She lifts and stares into my eyes, searching for something—although I'm not sure what. "Anywhere I want to go?"

I smooth her hair back from her cheek and smile. "Anywhere."

"What are your parents doing for Christmas?"

I frown, my hand dropping from her hip as my mind races in a million directions. I'm offering her an escape to anywhere her heart desires and she's asking about my family in South Dakota? "My parents?"

She bites her lip and drops her eyes from mine. "Maybe that's too forward..."

I hook my finger under her chin and bring her gaze back to mine. "It's not too forward, but I was envisioning you in a bikini on a beach, not in a flannel and boots playing in the snow outside of Rapid City."

"Is that where you're from?"

"Yeah." I chuckle. "You really want to spend Christmas with my parents?"

She nods. "I haven't had a family Christmas in five years. Then last year I spent it alone, but at least I talked to Chad on the phone. This year... well, I was prepared to be truly alone for the first time, but then you came for me."

I think about calling my mom—her shrieking over the phone as she yells at my dad to go back to the store for supplies. "My mother will love you forever if we spend Christmas with them."

"Really?"

"Nothing would make her happier."

"Do we leave in the morning?"

I cup her face and kiss her deeply while rolling my hips underneath her, letting her know how hard and needy I am for her. "I have a meeting tomorrow at a kennel, and then I'd like to take you out on a proper date, but we can go the day after if that's cool with you."

"A kennel?"

"Yeah." I sigh. "A couple of my old unit members—the K9 handlers—established a training facility here in Spring City. One of the guys has been pushing me to stop by and talk to the owner about a PTSD support dog."

"Did these guys know Chad?"

I nod. "At least one of them did."

Here I lie with a beautiful and naked woman on top of me, the wet heat from her pussy calling to my cock, and both of our heads are somewhere else.

"I can't believe there were people here in town that knew my brother, and I never thought to look for them."

"They offered to reach out to you, but I said no." I brush her hair back. "I had to get my shit together and come to you myself. It had to be me. But now I think that might have been selfish."

She shakes her head. "No. I'm glad it was you."

"Would you go with me tomorrow?" I've been dodging Karden for months, and was a downright asshole while I was drinking, but he never gave up on me. I think that's the foster kid in him. He chooses his family and holds on tight. I owe it to him and anyone else who is there to show them I'm alive and kicking.

Better than alive and kicking, now that I've met Charity.

Survivor's guilt kept me from coming to her, but shame kept me from responding to my unit members.

Shame, because even though I was the one wounded and bleeding, I got to come home. Not them, though. They had to stay and continue to do the job like nothing happened—like two of their fellow soldiers hadn't fucking disappeared in a blink of an eye.

Karden, Saint, Hollywood, and a couple of other guys sent me emails and texts in the beginning, but I couldn't bring myself to respond. What the hell was I going to say to them?

My shoulder and knee fucking hurt and the bullshit pain meds the VA gave me don't do shit. My brain is all fucked up and I wake up in a cold, alcohol-infused sweat night after night. I don't have a real job and I'm living in my parent's basement because my mom has me on suicide watch even though I've never said anything to clue her into where my dark thoughts go sometime. I'm killing it as a civilian, guys. Thanks for asking.

Everyone took the hint after a few months, but not Karden. That bastard doesn't know when to give up. He's a stubborn ass mule that way, and the only reason he knows anything about my life is because he got my parent's phone number and talked to my mother.

I still don't know how he pulled off that one, considering their number isn't listed.

I was wrong about how I dismissed them while wallowing in self-pity. But now that I'm here, now that

I've met Charity and know she is meant to be mine, I feel strong enough to face my brethren again.

Especially if I have her at my side.

"I suppose it would be cathartic for me to meet people who knew Chad as Sergeant Miller."

"That's a good point."

"To be honest, I couldn't do it without you." Charity blushes and lays her cheek against my chest. This moment between us is so intimate—sex mixed with gut-churning emotion—that it's foreign and yet somehow comfortable. It's as if I innately know I will never be this vulnerable with another person.

Only Charity—my one and only.

She continues. "The Army offered me counseling in the beginning, but I turned them down. I wasn't ready back then, but after spending a couple hours with you, and hearing your stories, I feel closer to Chad than ever." She brings her head up and presses her lips to mine. "Thank you for giving me that."

"Damn. If I had known that meeting you would start to heal my heart and mind, I would have come months ago."

"Maybe sooner would have been too soon? Maybe we both needed time to be ready to accept each other?"

"You're very wise, you know that?"

She giggles and makes a funny face. "What do you say we take this to the bedroom and snuggle up under the covers?"

"Another smart idea. I like it."

VETERAN
K9
TEAM
REPORTING
FOR DUTY

Chapter 6
Charity

I wake up alone, the smell of coffee coming through the closed bedroom door from the kitchen. We fell asleep mid-conversation shortly after crawling into bed, the emotions of the day exhausting both of us.

Throughout the night, Bishop had a fitful sleep—twitching as if he was shaking off a bad dream. Each time, I wrapped my arms around him, threw my leg over his, pressed my cheek against his heart, and did my best to be his weighted blanket. He calmed instantly, his arms tightening and pulling me close like in the elevator, but he never woke up.

It was scary, and yet somehow sweet, as if I were made to be the balm to his tortured soul.

Considering I feel lighter this morning than I have in over a year, I'm thinking he's the balm for my broken and battered soul, too.

I roll out of bed, noting the time before throwing on my robe and stuffing my feet into my fuzzy slippers. Shuffling into the living room/kitchen, I smile when Bishop brings his eyes up from his phone. "Good morning."

He sets his phone down and comes around the island to pull me against his hard body. He's shirtless, wearing only his boxer shorts, his skin warm despite the cooler temperature of the winter morning. "Yes it is, angel. A very good morning."

"How long have you been up?"

"A couple of hours." Considering it's only eight, I have to wonder if he is an early riser, or if his inability to sleep has something to do with his dreams.

"Did you not sleep okay?"

"I slept great. Probably the best I have in a year. Did you?"

"Yes." I wrap my arms around him and press a kiss to his sternum. "Were you working out?"

"Just a few push-ups and sit-ups to wake myself up. I hope you don't mind that I helped myself and made coffee."

"I don't mind at all. Did you leave me a cup?"

"Of course, but I'll make you a fresh pot if you don't like it. We drink it strong and black in the military."

"That's exactly how I like it before I doctor it up with sweetener and cream." He hands me a hot cup, and I fix it the way I like with my sugar-free syrups and half-and-half. Bishop watches my process carefully, and I'm guessing he'll be making me my coffee tomorrow. The idea alone is enough to make me swoon.

I take my first sip and sigh contently, smiling up at him. "What time are we heading to the kennels?"

He tilts his head toward his phone. "I got a text from Karden. He said this afternoon would be best—somewhere around two. I guess Hollywood is in town and he'll be there."

"Hollywood?"

"Yeah, he was with me and your brother when..."

I nod my understanding. "I think I would like to meet him, too."

Bishop pulls me into his arms, and it's easy for me to believe that I am his security blanket. He puts his chin on top of my head and sighs, holding me tightly. "I've barely talked to these guys since I left theater. So, this could turn into an emotional day or a fight. Really, it could go either way."

"I'm here for you, no matter what. Together, we'll be fine."

"You really are a fucking angel, you know that? My angel." Bishop pulls back and looks me in the eye. "What do you say to a hot shower, followed by a belly filling late breakfast?"

"Are we showering together?" I arch my brow.

He grins. "Abso-fucking-lutely."

"Then I say let's do it, but I need five minutes of privacy first." My morning pee hits me and I remember that I still haven't brushed my teeth. Yeesh!

He nods. "Take your time and open the door when you're ready for me to join you."

I pull out of his arms, take another deep drink of my coffee, and set the half-empty mug down on the counter. "We should stop by your hotel and check you out. No reason for you to pay for a room that you're not staying in."

"Good point." He swats my butt with an open hand, and it sends tingles vibrating through my body. "Go on."

Running into my bathroom, I take care of business and quickly brush my teeth before shedding my robe and turning on the shower. I crack open the door, and then step under the spray, running the soap over my body in between my legs.

The glass shower door opens and Bishop's gorgeously naked body steps in, his dick half hard. Even though he got me off twice last night, when we crawled into bed together, we never took the opportunity to truly admire each other.

I plan to rectify that this morning, and I hope he likes the way I touch him. To be honest, I don't think I'm very good at giving head. My last boyfriend said I sucked at it —not a pun—and waved me off anytime I reached for him. Maybe that was because I didn't really want to with him, but with Bishop...

I want to.

Lathering my hands, I run them all over Bishop's muscled chest, sliding lower over the ridges of his abdomen until I'm unapologetically wrapping my fingers around his thick cock. Bishop lets out a low groan and closes his eyes for a second before opening them, his dark blue eyes near black with desire. As I stroke his length, I smile and kneel, keeping my eyes on his.

His lips part as he sucks in his breath. "Are you going to wrap those pretty lips around me, angel?"

I answer by sticking out my tongue and swirling the head of his cock. "You worshiped me last night, and now it's my turn to worship you."

Bishop shakes his head and runs his finger through my wet hair. "Charity, I haven't begun to worship you."

"Mmmm." I take him as deep as I can, his fingers flexing against my scalp, his thumb caressing my cheekbone as I close my eyes and draw him in and out of my mouth.

No man has ever touched me with such reverence—as if I was the most precious thing on the planet—and I wonder if he's always been like this or if I'm special? Does this feel like something more to him, as it does me? I'm trying not to get ahead of myself, but there have already been too many sweet, heartfelt things said to not have my head in the clouds. I truly believe Chad brought us together at exactly the right time, when we were both open and ready to receive each other.

Sounds woo-woo, I know, but it's who I am—who I've always been.

"Look at me, Charity." Bishop commands in a tone I've yet heard him use—guttural, almost pained.

I open my eyes, pulling my head back and dragging the tip of my tongue underneath his shaft. "No good?"

"Fucking amazing, but I want to be connected with you." He arches his brow. "Keep going."

His bossiness turns me on and I double down on my effort, licking and sucking until his fingers intertwine with my long strands and he's fisting my hair. "Fuck me. Stop. Stand up."

"What?"

He helps me to my feet and presses my back against the cool tile wall, claiming my lips in a forceful kiss that eliminates any concerns I had. Not only does he like my skills, he loves them. He slides his hand between my legs, his middle finger finding and circling my clit before slipping inside of me. "Good, you're wet."

"Yes, I am."

"Did sucking my cock get you hot, angel?"

"You liking it did."

Bishop chuckles. "I'm thinking our bodies were made for each other. Put your arms around my neck. I'm going to lift you."

"What?" I ask again, but he doesn't hesitate, sliding his powerful forearms behind my thighs and lifting me in the air. "Bishop!"

"Hold on to me." He adjusts slightly and pins me to the wall with his chest while guiding his cock to my wet and desperate pussy. One smooth thrust and he fills me like no other, my body vibrating with pleasure.

"Oh!" I moan, burying my face into his neck as he pumps his hips, jack-hammering into me and rubbing against my g-spot perfectly until I'm on the verge of coming. "Oh god, Bishop."

I come apart seconds before he groans, pushing deep inside of me, his cock jerking as he comes. "Fuck."

My legs shake, or maybe it's his forearms, or both, as we pant to catch our breaths. "Put me down, Bishop. I'm heavy."

He kisses my forehead and pulls back to look me in the eye. "You're perfect."

I smile. "That might be, but you should still put me down."

Begrudgingly, he sets me down, my legs wobbly underneath me. He pulls me into his chest and turns me under the spray that is quickly losing its heat. "Do I need to wash your hair?"

"No. I'll just throw it up in a braid."

We quickly soap up and rinse off, and jump out of the shower. Bishop hands me my robe and wraps a towel around his waist. "Now, I'm hungry."

"Glad I could help you work up an appetite."

He pulls me into his arms one more time. It's like he can't stop himself from touching me, which suits me just fine. "Angel, you are my appetite."

After grabbing his stuff and checking Bishop out of his hotel, we stop at the Five and Dime Diner downtown for some old-fashioned home cooking. This place—a Spring City staple from fifty years ago—was our favorite place to go as kids. Once we are both overly full, we take a drive and I navigate us to the home Chad and I grew up in, thirty minutes south of Spring City. We park at my old high school and walk hand-in-hand around the football field like a couple in love.

It's strangely comforting to share this piece of my past with someone who loved Chad almost as much as I did.

A little before two, we drive to the Veteran K9 Center and head down a dirt road to a trio of metal buildings east of Spring City. There are a handful of trucks and cars in a makeshift parking lot, and when we exit the vehicle, we hear dogs barking in the distance.

I meet Bishop at the front of his truck, and once again he takes my hand, claiming me as his, or maybe proclaiming us as a couple.

Regardless of his intention, it warms me all the way to my toes. I squeeze his hand to reassure him. "We got this."

"Yeah."

We walk through the door of the middle building at the same time a big guy with biceps the size of my head walks out of an office with a Shepherd at his side. "Can I help you?"

"I'm—" Bishop clears his throat. "I'm looking for Karden."

Two guys, one tall and tattooed, the other blond and beautiful, come out of the office.

"Holy shit, man." The beautiful one eats up the distance between us in three long steps and pulls Bishop into his arms.

Bishop pauses and then drops my hand, wrapping his arms around the guy.

The tall one approaches and offers me his hand. At the same time, a handful of other people come out of the office. "How are you doing? I'm Karden."

I take his hand and try to smile. "Charity."

Bishop pulls away from the other guy and wraps his arm around my waist. "Guys, this is Charity Miller."

Adding my last name changes the air in the room as both men's eyes swing to me and they slowly nod their head in understanding.

"Miller," the beautiful one says. "I'm Logan."

"Hollywood," Bishop says, putting all the pieces together for me.

"Nice to meet you both," I say through a shaky breath.

Crap, this is harder than I thought it would be.

VETERAN
K9
TEAM
REPORTING
FOR DUTY

Chapter 7
Bishop

I don't know what I was expecting, but the greeting I got from Hollywood was not it. That was a hug born of relief—plain and simple. I offer Karden my hand, but he smacks it away and pulls me into his chest, his arms wrapping around my back and squeezing me in a bear hug. The guy is a couple inches taller than me, but I'm betting we're closer matched now than the last time we saw each other considering the muscle I've put on.

"You look good, man. Better than I expected." Never one to hold back, Karden arches his brow to give me ten months of shit with that one look. And then the scolding is over. He motions to the crowd that has assembled behind him. "Come meet everyone."

I recognize a couple of the guys, although I'm unsure of their names. We must have crossed paths at some point or another, but I'm not sure when and where.

Karden starts with the Viking with the red beard and

thick biceps. "This is Kemp, Vale, Barron, and Linc. And Janey is around here somewhere."

I shake hands with each of them, and then watch as they respectfully introduce themselves to Charity. I'm guessing Karden told them about Miller, and hearing her last name was enough to clue them in.

"Would you like something to drink?" Hollywood asks Charity, pointing to a coffee cabinet in the corner of their office. "They have coffee, hot cocoa, soda, and water."

"No, thanks." She shakes her head and smiles sweetly. Instinctively, I grab her hand again and interlace our fingers. I can't seem to stop myself from touching her, as if tethered together is the only lifeline I have.

Hopefully, I'm her lifeline, too.

"We also have beer, if you want," Linc offers.

I shake my head. "None for me, but thanks."

Karden stares at me, as if he's reliving the last ten months of my life with that one statement. "Good for you, man."

"Where's Kiki?" I segue into lighter topics.

He grins. "She's with the puppies. Want to meet them?"

"Puppies?" Charity chirps and squeezes my fingers. All the anxiety of the situation melts away, and I bring her hand to my mouth and kiss her fingers.

Karden and Hollywood exchange a look and turn toward the door that muffles the barking on the other end.

Charity and I follow them through the door that

leads to a large indoor arena with artificial turf and agility training equipment. Kiki, a Belgian Malinois, and a Rottweiler that I don't recognize look up from their position outside of a black chain-link kennel. Karden utters a command and Kiki runs toward us, sitting down two steps in front of him.

I chuckle and carefully take a knee, waiting until he releases her to come to me. We spent many nights wrestling and cuddling on the floor of Karden's connex while deployed. "Hey Kiki. Remember me?"

"She remembers you." He releases her and she comes right to me, pushing her head against my chest.

"Awww. Good girl." I run my hands over her short coat as a petite blonde walks toward us with the Rottweiler.

"Welcome." She nods to me and Charity.

"Bishop, this is Janey LaVey. She started the VKC and recruited all of us to join her," Karden says.

I stand and offer her my hand. "Nice to meet you. This is Charity."

She shakes my hand and then shakes Charity's. "Would you like to meet our puppies?"

"Yes, please." Charity practically bounces on her toes.

Chuckling, we follow Janey to a pen of four Rottweiler puppies. Charity drops to a crouch, cooing at the pups who climb over each other to grab her attention. "Awww. They are so cute."

"Is this the momma?" I motion to the big girl with the bucket head.

Janey shakes her head and strokes her dog's flank. "No, but they are from the same line. Technically, she's their older sister. This is my dog, Macha."

"She's beautiful."

"Can I pick them up?" Charity asks cautiously, glancing over her shoulder as the puppies nibble on her fingers.

"Absolutely. The pen is clean. Take a seat and let them climb all over you."

I join Charity in the six-by-six box with the hard foam mat floor—carefully lowering myself to the ground and stretching out my injured knee—and let the puppies check us out. At first they are cautious, but it takes less than a minute for them to lose their fear and crawl all over us. They are cute, but it's the feisty one tugging on my pant leg that I'm most enamored by.

Janey laughs. "Looks like one of them picked you."

"What exactly does that mean?" Karden mentioned a PTSD program, and while I've heard of combat veteran support animals, I know nothing about them.

I glance up at Karden before swinging my gaze at Janey.

She shrugs and turns her attention back to Karden.

He grins. "It means, if you're interested, you could be our first veteran to run through our program."

"Where do you live?" Janey asks.

I glance at Charity, who is looking at me expectantly with her brow raised. We haven't talked about this yet, but I've already decided I'm moving here. There's no way in hell I can leave her side now, and will only do so if she tells me to go away. Even then, it would be hard to walk away. "I currently live in Rapid City, but I'm thinking about moving here after the holidays."

Charity flashes me a beautiful smile, letting me know she is on board with having me close.

How close is something we still need to discuss.

"That's good." Janey nods her approval. "The program is new, and while we don't have to have the veteran on site to train full time with the support animal, I think it would be nice to ease into the program with somebody local."

"What kind of work are you looking for when you get here?" Hollywood leans against the chain link with his hands in his pockets.

I shrug, my heart lodging itself in my throat. "I don't know, man. When I do work, it's at my old man's hardware store. I haven't figured out what's next yet. All I know is it will be here."

Turning my eyes to the puppy crawling into my lap, the same one who was pulling on my pant leg a minute ago, I pick him up and pin his squiggly body to my chest.

Fuck me—here's that fucking shame coming back to rear its ugly head. I can't look my brethren in the eyes while I tell them I've been a worthless piece of shit living in my parent's basement for the last eight months while I was dodging their phone calls.

It's not that I don't have money, because I do. I was medically retired, so I get a VA disability check every month for the rest of my life—but to date, I haven't figured out what I'm going to do with that life.

Now that I've met Charity, I know it has to be something meaningful that I can be proud of—that will also make her proud to call me her man.

"We should talk," Hollywood says. "It's time to catch you up on what's going on, especially if you're going to move here."

His words remind me that Hollywood wasn't a K9 handler—he was a grunt like me. I raise my head and pin him with an arched brow. "What are you doing here? You weren't K9."

He grins. "Remember all the rumors about me? The reason you call me Hollywood?"

"Not really." I narrow my eyes, trying to remember the exact stories told about him. Something about him being related to an actor or something, although I can't remember if he ever said which one. He looks like many of them with his expensive taste, blond hair, green eyes, and rugged good looks.

"They were true. I'm separating from the Army right now and moving here myself. Karden pulled me out here to meet Janey, who invited me to invest in the future of the VKC, and part of that is starting my enterprise—" he shrugs "—the Mejer Veteran K9 Stunt Academy, and I'm going to need help once we get started in January."

"Okay..." I have no idea what he's talking about, but if he wants to offer me a job, I'm willing to listen.

"We can talk about it after you move here." Hollywood smiles.

"Of course that means you have to answer your

fucking phone when we call." Karden raises his brow with a sarcastic tilt to his lips.

"Fuck you." I roll my eyes and chuckle. It feels good to talk shit with them, because this is the way it was in the field. We had to fuck with each other, otherwise we wouldn't survive six to twelve months in the middle of nothingness. Messing with each other was the only way to pass the time when there was nothing else going on, and as I told Charity last night, Miller and I were the chief mischief-makers.

The puppy in my arms has fallen to sleep. I glance down at him with his round, well-fed belly and then over to Charity, who is watching us with tears in her eyes. Concern laces through me, and I reach out to touch her, sliding my fingers on top of her thigh. "What's the matter, baby?"

"Nothing. I just—" she shakes her head and bites her lip "—listening to you guys give each other a hard time, I can imagine Chad here with his derpy smile cracking jokes that only he finds funny."

Hollywood sighs, a wistful smile spreading his lips. "Miller was hilarious when he wasn't messing with you."

"Yeah, but you never knew when he was going to come get you. He kept us on our toes." Karden chuckles, "He was a good guy. We miss him."

Hollywood nods but says nothing more.

I turn my gaze back to Charity, who is smiling at them. The silence is perfect, a moment of reverence for our fallen brother, interrupted only by a squeak and then a yip as one puppy goes after another. Meanwhile, the one in my arms stays blissfully unaware and deep in slumber.

Janey finally breaks the silence. "We should name the little guy. Any ideas?"

Chuckling, I bring my eyes up to Hollywood and Karden, both of them nodding with grins on their faces.

We say it at the same time, "Jester."

"Jester?" Charity asks, her eyes bouncing between us but settling on me.

"It was our nickname for Miller during our last deployment." I lean forward, hand her the sleeping puppy, and kiss her cheek.

She sighs and hugs him close to her heart. "It's perfect."

Reaching out to Karden, I let him pull me to my feet, and then I step out of the pen. "How do we get started?"

Janey motioned to the offices we started in. "We have some paperwork for you to sign, but we can handle all that after you move to town."

"It'll be good to have you here." Karden puts his big hand on my shoulder and squeezes.

I nod, relief seeping through my bones, settling my mind and my heart. "It'll be good to be here."

VETERAN
K9
TEAM

REPORTING
FOR DUTY

Chapter 8
Charity

I wake up the next morning blissfully sore after making love to Bishop all night long. And it was making love, because sex has never left me so satisfied.

From the living room, I hear Bishop on his phone. "We'll be home in time for dinner."

...

"Yeah, it went fine."

...

"No, you don't have to make up the spare room for her."

...

"Because she's not staying at the house."

...

"Whatever you make will be fine. I'll see you tonight."

Bishop turns around to find me standing under the threshold of my bedroom. "Good morning, angel."

I try to flash him a smile, but it doesn't quite reach my eyes as the conversation with his mother runs through my mind.

What was I thinking, asking to meet his family after one night?

Not even one night, one orgasm.

One orgasm and I'm asking to meet his mother.

What is wrong with me?

"Good morning." I squeak.

His brow furrows, and he glances at the phone in his hand. "What's wrong?"

I shake my head, but my tongue betrays me. "Do I need to make a hotel reservation?"

"Oh." He smiles knowingly and walks toward me, slipping his phone into his pocket. "My mother means well, but after the last two nights, it's going to be hard enough keeping my hands off you during dinner. I don't feel like staying quiet while I sneak into your room at night. Besides, I didn't think you'd want me telling her you'll be sleeping with me from here on out."

I exhale the breath I'm holding and smile. "What are we going to tell your family?"

He shrugs, running his hands up my arms. "I thought we'd discuss that on the drive out there."

"What do you want to tell them?"

"Me?" He pulls me into his arms and kisses my temple. "I want to tell them I'm an asshole for waiting for so long to come see you. That if I had come six months ago when I first got home, we'd already be engaged and planning our wedding."

My head snaps back and I glance up at him with wide eyes. "You feel it too—this connection between us?"

"I feel it. I keep wondering what this Christmas would have been like if Chad had made it home. Did he know we were perfect for each other? Would he have sanctioned our relationship? If not, would his disapproval have stopped me from pursuing you?" Bishop shrugs again. "I don't know. What I do know is that I'd like to walk into my parent's house with you on my arm, your hand in mine. I don't want to hide how I feel about you, because honestly, I'm not sure I can."

"Maybe we do what feels natural regardless of what other people expect."

He smiles. "I like that."

Seven hours later, we're pulling up to a cute little suburban two-story with a detached garage. An attractive blonde woman in a festive sweater vest and red turtleneck comes bounding out of the house with Golden Retriever energy, clapping her hands like a wild woman whose name was just called on the Price is Right.

He groans. "I should have warned you."

I giggle. "She's adorable."

Bishop's mom comes to my side of the truck, swinging my door open before I can unbuckle my seatbelt.

"Oh my word, you are gorgeous!" She pulls me into

her arms as soon as my feet hit concrete, and for a little woman, she's got one hell of a grip. I have no choice but to wrap my arms around her and return the hug.

"Hello Mrs, uh, Bishop." It's at that moment I realize I have no idea the first name of the man who was cock-deep inside me eight hours ago.

"Call me Connie." She pulls back and gives me a huge smile. "Or Mom. You can call me Mom."

"Let's bring it down about thirty percent, Mom," Bishop calls from the driver's side. "We don't want to scare her off before she steps foot into the house."

"Pish-posh." His mother waves away his warning and brings her eyes back to me. "I'm so happy you came. Liam says it was your idea to spend Christmas with us?"

Liam. Bishop's name is Liam? Short for William, maybe?

I nod slowly when I realize she's waiting for a response. "Yes. I thought it would be nice to spend Christmas with a family for a change."

Connie presses her lips together, tears forming in her eyes. "Oh, you sweet girl, I'm so sorry about your brother. We've heard such wonderful things about him."

"For Christ's sake, Mom." Bishop interlaces his fingers with mine and pulls me back a step from his mother.

"It's okay, Connie. I appreciate you hitting the topic head on."

"Connie, your stew is bubbling." An older version of Bishop stands at the door, giving me a glimpse into how handsome my man will be in another twenty to thirty years. The older man waves and gives us an exasperated head bob.

"Then turn off the burner, Bill," she snaps with a smile on her face.

"Would you come inside and let the kids have a minute to breathe?" he snaps back with a smirk that tells me bickering is a form of loving communication between them.

Bishop leans down and whispers in my ear. "It's not too late, you know. I'm just saying: you in a bikini on the beach in south Florida. Me rubbing lotion over every inch of your body—"

I giggle and bump him in the ribs with my elbow.

A sly smile comes over Connie's face as she notices our interlaced fingers and the blush blooming on my cheeks. "Grab your bags and come inside."

"I told you, Mom. Charity's not staying here."

"Don't be ridiculous. I've already put fresh sheets and towels in the basement. It's far enough away from our bedroom to afford you plenty of privacy." The heat in my cheeks rises as Connie gives me a knowing wink. Then she walks away as if her word is final.

Bishop grumbles. "Get back in the truck and we'll make a break for it."

"Stop." I chuckle and turn to face him, a huge smile on my face. "She's adorable. Slightly nuts, maybe, but it's obvious that you being home means the world to her."

"It's not just me being here." Bishop wraps his arms

around me, pulling me tight against his body. "Like I said during the drive, I've been living with my folks since I separated from the military. I could've gotten my own place, but it would've killed her if I'd moved out before I had my shit straight. She's asked about you many times over the last few months, and knew that you were my last loose end before I was ready to start the next phase of my life." He strokes my cheek with his fingers. "Now, I know you are the next phase of my life, and I think she knows it, too."

"I'm glad you came for me, although I wish we had met a different way. It's like a convoluted dream—a nightmare that turns into a romance. I'm afraid I'm going to wake up and only half of it will be true." Whispering, I admit my worst fear. I don't doubt the words coming from Bishop's mouth, anymore than I doubt my own feelings, which are just as strong and overwhelming, but I do fear this is a dream, and when I wake up the good parts won't have happened.

No Bishop.

No goo seeping into all the cracks of my broken heart, making me feel warm and safe and loved—as if I'm on the path to being whole again. Or as whole as I can be without Chad.

"Me, too." He leans forward and presses his forehead against mine. "You're too good to be real, angel."

"But I am real." I tilt my face up and capture his mouth in a sweet kiss that turns hot the moment his tongue swipes along my bottom lip. He pulls me closer and tilts his head, deepening our kiss. Within seconds, we're pulling each other even closer, our bodies taking over from our exhausted minds.

"Fuck dinner," he growls.

Using every ounce of strength and willpower I have, I push him back. "Let's grab our bags and bask in the warmth of a Bishop family Christmas, Liam." I enunciate his name, my lips curling into a wicked smirk. Lowering my voice, I lean into him. "I can't believe I rode your cock last night without knowing your first name."

"Don't put that image in my head right now. You rode me like an angel, and I'm hard thinking about it." Bishop steps back and opens the rear door of his quad cab truck. He grabs both our bags and slings them over his shoulder, nodding his head toward the house. "Speaking of which, we should talk about birth control."

"I'm on the pill." I whisper as we walk to the front door. Right before I step up on the stoop, his father lets me know we have an audience by swinging open the screen door.

"Come on in, little lady." Mr. Bishop offers me his hand. "It's really nice to have you here."

I shake his hand. "Thank you for having me."

Bishop says from behind me, "Dad, this is Charity. Charity, this is Bill Bishop."

From the kitchen, his mom yells, "Or you can call him Dad!"

Both men roll their eyes and shake their heads, and I see the family resemblance. Giggling, I lower my voice. "We have Bill and Liam, but is it really William senior and junior?"

"Smart woman." Bill flashes a smile at his son. "I like her."

"Yeah," Bishop says, smiling down at me, "I like her, too."

"Wash up. It's time to eat," Connie calls from the dining room table as she sets down a stack of plates.

"This way, baby." Bishop descends a set of stairs into a fully furnished basement the size of the upstairs. It's got its own living room, bedroom, and bathroom.

"Wow. This is bigger than my apartment."

He shrugs and glances around. "I'd say it's about the same size."

"Is this where you've been living?" I look around, noting the free weights and benches against one wall.

"Since I got out of the hospital. I plan to get a real job and then move out. Like I said, I was waiting to get through the holidays."

"And get through me." I bat my eyelashes.

He puts our bags down and pulls me into his arms. "Get to you. There's a difference."

"And now you're stuck with me for the holidays."

"I hope it's for a lot longer than that."

I stare into his eyes, seeing nothing but love and sincerity. I could deny what I'm feeling, the warmth simmering in my chest as my heart swells with love for this man, but why?

Why throw stones at a new and fragile glass house before the foundation cures?

Why can't I have this, even if it's absolutely crazy?

Whirlwind romances happen, don't they?

"I hope so, too."

A wicked gleam is in his eyes as his gaze trails over my body, causing goosebumps to break out on my arms and my nipples to pebble under my bra. "Let's go eat so I can feign exhaustion and get you alone again."

VETERAN
K9
TEAM
REPORTING
FOR DUTY

Chapter 9
Bishop

"Would you like to go to the salon and get a mani-pedi tomorrow?"

Charity looks at her chipped nail polish and then at me before bringing her eyes to my mom. "That would be great. I'm overdue."

My mom claps her hands. "Wonderful. I've always wanted a daughter to go with me to the salon."

"What are you talking about? I've gone with you twice in the last four months." I scoff, shoving half a roll into my mouth.

"You get pedicures?" Charity raises her eyebrow in my direction.

I shrug. "Sometimes."

Her smile is a mile wide. "Chad went with me a few times while he was home on leave. I loved how my big, badass brother would be the only guy sitting in the middle of a row of chicks. It didn't faze him in the slightest to be the only man. If anything, I think he scored a couple of phone numbers from our spa dates."

Chuckling, I admit, "My first pedicure was with Chad. It was during our first deployment while we were in Qatar. We booked massages, pedicures, haircuts, and shaves. They know how to do it at the R&R sites."

"The guys didn't mess with you and Chad about having a spa day?"

"Hell, no. After they saw the women pampering us, they scrambled to make their own appointments before our seventy-two hours were up." I throw her a wink.

"Well, you're not invited," my mom pipes in. "This is a girls' shopping trip."

I glance between my mom and dad, but know my parents well enough to know arguing is futile. I'm not sure what my mom is up to, but I wouldn't be able to stop her if I did know, so maybe it's better I don't ask questions. "Fine. Dad and I will go do something manly, like throw axes at plywood."

"Oh! That sounds fun, too." Charity chuckles.

"That does sound fun," Mom muses.

"Good grief," my dad grumbles. "I am not putting an ax in your hands, woman."

Charity laughs and leans back in her chair, one hand on her wine glass, the other resting on her belly. A flash of what could be hits me as I imagine her swollen with my child. Do I want children? I hadn't thought about it much before, but at this moment I know with Charity I do. With her, I want everything.

"That was so good, Connie. You'll have to teach me how to make it."

"Sure thing. I'll teach you all of Liam's favorite foods." My mom also leans back in her chair.

I stand up and put my hand on Charity's plate. "All done?"

"I'll do the dishes." She leans forward to put her wine glass down.

My dad also stands up and shakes his head, putting his hand up in the air. "In this house, Connie cooks and I clean."

Mom smiles and lifts her wine glass to her lips. "It's a good deal because Bill can't cook for shit."

He leans down and kisses the top of my mom's head. "And my beautiful bride can't clean for shit."

She laughs and winks at Charity. "That's totally true."

Charity sits back in her chair. "Far be it from me to mess with a Bishop family tradition."

I gather a stack of plates and silverware and walk into the kitchen with my dad at my back. Dad turns on the faucet, which drowns out my mom's voice right as I hear her say, "Can I tell you a story, Charity?"

Glancing at my dad, I lower my voice. "Can I trust what's going on in the other room?"

He smiles, his eyes on the task at hand. "You're in love," he states rather than asks.

"Is that insane?" I lean my ass against the counter and cross my arms over my chest. I've never felt an ounce of what I'm feeling right now for any woman I've ever dated, and that includes my on-again, off-again high school sweetheart.

"I knew the moment I locked eyes with your mother that she was the one. Before we were introduced, before we exchanged names, before our first kiss, I knew I was going to spend the rest of my life with her." He shuts off the water and turns toward me, his eyes full of warmth and wisdom. "Connie knew it, too. Neither of us can explain it, but I believe sometimes the universe lets you know by presenting you with an opportunity and saying 'don't fuck this up'. I'm betting your mom is telling your lady the same story right now."

C harity covers her mouth and stifles the cry ripping from her throat as her orgasm crashes over her.

I lift my head from between her thighs, wiping her juices from my mouth. "I fucking love how you taste."

"I've never come so hard in my life," she says after catching her breath.

I settle my body between her legs and rest my chin between her breasts. "My parents love you."

She glances down at me, running her fingers gently through my hair. "You have a great family. Thank you for sharing them with me."

Her eyes are shiny, smile sweet, cheeks flushed—and she's the most beautiful fucking thing I've ever seen. Like an angel, only better, because she's here, and she's real, and she's mine. I swallow the lump in my throat and go for broke. "And I love you."

Her breath hitches and her hands still in my hair. Then her lips spread into a dazzling smile. "I love you, too."

I move up and capture her lips in a passionate kiss that relays every raw emotion pumping through my veins. She welcomes me in, spreading her legs wider so my hard cock is nestled against her slick folds. I slide into her slowly, wanting to feel every ridge of her pussy as it clamps down around me. Charity fits me perfectly, like a puzzle piece I never knew I was missing, and my heart swells with a love I didn't know I was capable of feeling.

She tightens around me, and I know her climax is close by the way her fingers press insistently into my shoulders.

"Come for me, angel."

She mewls, her pussy gripping me tight, milking me for the release I'm on the verge of giving her. Pumping my hips harder, faster, I wonder if she can orgasm twice in a row before my brain disconnects and my release takes over. I bury my face in her neck, words tumbling out of my mouth. "I want this forever."

She wraps her arms around me and holds me in a tight embrace as she whispers in my hair, "Me, too."

"I am moving to Spring City after the holidays," I restate with absolute surety. "I wasn't just saying that yesterday."

"You'll move in with me," she replies with the same no-nonsense confidence.

I lift my head and look her in the eye. "You'd be okay with that?"

She grins. "Let's be honest with ourselves. We're going to be in each other's bed every night anyway, so why pay rent twice?"

"Practical and beautiful." I place a sweet kiss on her lips and roll off her, pulling her into my arms. "Your apartment building is fairly fancy for my Midwest ass."

She rests her head on my chest and trails her fingers over my abs. "Yeah, but it's got a gym, pool, hot tub, and sauna on the second floor, as well as security, two parking spaces, and a private dog park."

"Perfect for Jester."

"Perfect for us."

"Of course, we'll need to find a house eventually. The kids will want their own rooms." I slide the topic of family into the conversation, testing out the idea on her.

"How many kids do you want—Mister Only Child?" She giggles. "Or should I ask Connie how many grand-kids she wants?"

"Good lord. If you ask her, she's going to tell you a dozen."

"I don't think you'll like my ass much after birthing a dozen kids."

"I will always love your ass, but I don't want to share you that much. Growing up, I always wanted a brother or sister, so I'm picking two. What about you?"

"At least three. Maybe four, depending upon how far apart they are in age."

"So, you've thought about this?"

"Of course I have. I work with kids. The great thing about Chad and I—we were only two years apart. Far enough that we had our own friends and did our own thing, but close enough that we could still relate to each other, could still enjoy each other, and some of our friends could be shared. Any further apart, and I think I would've been the annoying little sister to him.

Although to be honest, sometimes I still was for fun. And he was sometimes the jerk-face big brother."

"Do you think he's staring down at us—happy with how things are playing out?"

"At this exact moment, I hope not." Charity lifts her head and smiles, shimmying her naked body against mine. "But in general? Yeah, I do."

I think about that for a minute. My family isn't overly religious, and I'd never given the afterlife much thought before losing Jester, or more to the point, before meeting Charity.

It's too much for me to dwell on right now, but maybe something to come back to in the future.

"Love you." I kiss Charity's forehead and settle my hand on her hip.

"I love you, too." She presses a kiss to my chest and lies her head down over my heart. Within minutes, she's breathing softly, cajoling me to join her in sleep.

Hours later, I wake from a dream, but this one differs from my recurring one over the last ten months. Reminiscent of a beer commercial, Jester and I are lounging on a white sandy beach with Coronas in our hand. Sweet BBQ pineapple fills the air, its scent mixing perfectly with mild coconut and tart citrus. The sun is hot, but the breeze is cool as we stare out at the clear blue water. Soft feminine laughter comes from Jester's right side. We both look over before he turns to me, a goofy smile splitting his face.

"Here comes trouble."

I glance over him at Charity walking toward us with a tray piled high with food. "I love her, man."

He nods, his eyes still on her. "I knew you would."

"I'm going to marry her."

Jester turns to look at me, his eyebrow cocked. "You better."

"And I'll take care of her. She'll never want for anything. I promise."

"I know, man. I always knew."

I stare into his brown eyes, the small scar in his eyebrow causing the hair to grow in different directions. "Miss you."

"I'm right here, but—" he waggles his brows "—it's time to let me go, brother."

Turning my attention back to Charity, the tray of food is now a child, and the heaviness in my chest dissipates as a bone deep smile takes over my face. Jester's chair is empty, but his protective presence remains. I smile up at my woman, my heart so full of love for the two standing in front of me, it's on the verge of bursting.

"There are my angels."

VETERAN
K9
TEAM
REPORTING
FOR DUTY

Epilogue
Bishop - Four Months Later

"K9 Stunt Academy. What can I do for you?" I glance at the caller ID and note the 310 area code. No one that we know, because Hollywood is adamant we save known numbers. Apparently A-listers get quite offended when you don't know who they are, not that he cares. What he's doing is building our ignore list, which I find hilarious. Must be nice to have the freedom to refuse work.

I've been here for a little over three months now, and I'm pretty much his right hand man. Considering neither of us know what we are doing—buying land, managing general contractors, running a K9 stunt academy—and are learning as we go, I suppose I'm his perfect match. I know he's paying me way more than I'm worth, but when I brought it up, he shut that shit down quick with something like, "*No Purple Heart-wearing war hero is working for minimum wage. Get over it.*"

So... there's that.

I listen to the person on the other end. It's a woman

who claims we are abusing our dogs by making them jump off walls and leap onto fully grown men. We're profiting off their labor—their pain and suffering—and we're horrible human beings because of it.

What she doesn't understand is these are the happiest dogs I've ever seen. They legitimately get to play all day long. And I'm not just talking about the new ones being trained now, I'm talking about the ones that have been to war. Krieger, Kiki, Li-Lou, and the others. They have owners that spend twenty-three of the twenty-four hours of a day with them. They are living a better life than any Pomeranian purse pooch I know.

Unfortunately, this call is a weekly thing, although the caller is either changing up their phone number, or there's a network of them. This is the first one with an LA area code.

Bruce, who has partnered with us for the first three years to teach us the tricks of the movie-making trade, says it's part of doing business. "People care more about dogs than they do about the homeless vet they walk by sleeping on the street."

When he said that, it struck a nerve, and I've been struggling not to lash out at these callers ever since.

"Listen, lady. I'm going to tell you this once and only once. These dogs live a better life than you do. While your concern is admirable, it is misguided. Why don't you set your sights on puppy mills, or dog fighting operations, or the hoarder down the street with fifteen cats? Have a good day and don't call here again." I hang up and push a button that immediately routes her number through the ignore protocol, which means it won't ring here again. I don't exactly understand the technology, but apparently it won't let her leave voicemails either.

Perfect.

My cell phone dings with an incoming message. Considering the time, I know it's Charity letting me know she's done for the day and heading home.

Instead of texting, I call her back.

"Hello my love," she answers after the first ring.

A smile takes over my face. No matter what kind of day I'm having, the sound of her voice puts everything in perspective. I'm here. I'm alive. I'm in love. And I have the love and support of an amazing woman. "Hey, angel. How was your day?"

"Great. I'll tell you about Matilda's latest adventure when you get home."

I chuckle. "I love that little girl and her antics. What do you want for dinner?"

"Considering you expect me to wear a bikini on the beach in two days, I'm thinking soup and salad."

"First of all, you are absolute perfection. Secondly, we're staying in a house with a private beach—the bikini is optional. And lastly, that's rabbit food and I like feeding you. How about sushi?"

"Okay, but no squid chips." She giggles.

"No squid chips."

Three days later and we are in heaven. It is Charity's spring break so she's off from school, and we're on the tropical vacation we never got to take. We flew in this morning—taking the red eye out of Denver last night—and are staying in one of Hollywood's brothers' beach properties.

"This house is massive. Five bedrooms, seven bathrooms, pool, hot tub, and a private beach." Charity walks out of the house to the lanai in a bikini with a sarong tied around her waist. Holy shit, she takes my breath away every time. "So this is how the top one percent live?"

"I guess." I pull her into my arms and slide my palms over her ass, pulling her hips flush against mine.

Her eyes flash with heat. "Are you hard?"

"I am now."

"We've only been here fifteen minutes." She giggles, grinding her pussy against my cock.

"And?"

"Oh, I'm not complaining." She slides her hand between us and cups me through my board shorts. "Think they have hidden cameras in this house?"

"Yes, but it's a closed system and Levi had his cleaning people come out this morning to turn everything off. I got a text confirming it as soon as we touched down," I murmur against her neck, trailing kisses down between her breasts.

Charity slides her fingers into my hair and gently pushes my head down.

I chuckle and carefully drop to my knee, before rotating to my butt, and pulling her down on top of my face on the deck. Nothing turns me on more than when my woman tells me exactly what she wants and how she wants it. I find the ties on either side of her bottoms and pull, peeling the fabric away to find her pussy glistening with her arousal. "Mmmm. Someone else is turned on, too."

"I've been thinking about riding your mouth since we landed."

"Well then. Let's get started." I run my tongue up between her lower lips, smiling as she tosses her head back and moans. From day one, she's been responsive to me, only solidifying how perfect we are for each other.

Sucking her clit into my mouth, I grip her hips and help her grind her pussy against the scruff around my lips.

"Oh, Liam," she mewls, her thighs tightening as her orgasm crashes over. I continue to languidly lick and suck until she pulls away and pins me with her beautiful brown eyes. "So good."

"Yes, you are, angel."

Charity giggles and reaches behind her, rubbing her palm over my cock that is trapped underneath my shorts. She frees me and slides down my body, lining us up and sitting down to take me into her wet pussy. My eyes roll back in my head as I groan, her cunt warm and welcoming. "I will never get tired of how good you feel wrapped around me."

"No one fits me like you, fills me like you, makes love to me like you." Charity leans forward with her hands on my chest and presses a kiss to my lips. I lift my hips, quickening my pace, and fuck her from underneath. She buries her face into my neck as I push us both to the brink of releasing.

"Can you come for me again?" I pant, seconds away from climaxing myself.

"Yes," she moans, her cunt clamping down on me, sending me over the edge. I come hard, filling and marking her as mine again and again. Every time I come, I think about the day we'll be working on making a baby. I don't know why I'm in a hurry, but the image of her swollen with my child—the start of our perfect family life —calms every demon I've ever had.

I wrap my arms around her and pepper her shoulders with kisses. "Fucking love you so much, Charity."

"I love you, too."

"Want to take a swim?"

She lifts and smiles while untying her top before climbing off of me. "I guess there's no reason to wear this."

"None whatsoever." I tuck myself back into my shorts and accept her hand to help me to my feet. Kissing her forehead, I pat her bare butt and tilt my chin toward the pool. "I'll meet you there."

"Okay."

Epilogue

Back in the bedroom, I slip my hand into the secret pocket of my leather duffle bag. I was going to wait until a planned sailboat sunset cruise to do this, but something about this moment feels right. It's just like us from the moment we met. We gravitate toward each other, unable to keep our hands off each other—damn timing or decency.

I slip the ring my mother gave me—modified slightly with my own design—onto my pinkie and walk outside. Shucking off my shorts, I walk into the shallow pool and wade to the edge that overlooks the ocean. Charity is resting there, her forearms crossed and her chin resting on her hands. I swim up behind her, wrapping my arms around her with my chest pressed against her back.

"It's so beautiful," she muses, her gaze focused on the crystal clear water and white sandy beach.

"Yeah, it is." I kiss her cheek and put my hands on top of hers. "And so are you."

I know the moment she sees the ring. Her breathing hitches and there's a slight tremor in her arms. "What's that, Liam?"

"I'm hoping it's your engagement ring." I pull back so she can turn in my arms, her bottom lip trembling as her big, brown eyes fill with unshed tears. "You are heaven sent. My guardian angel. Even your name means kindness and compassion, of which you've shown me nonstop since the day we met. I love you more than I knew I could love someone, Charity, and in loving you, I've learned to love myself. You saved me when I thought there was nothing left to save, and I want nothing more than to take care of you—worship and love you—for the rest of our lives. Please, make me the happiest man to ever walk this earth and be my wife."

Charity shakes her head, but laughs and says, "Yes. Of course. What took you so long?"

I chuckle, sliding the ring onto her finger. "My mom gave me this ring while we were home for Christmas, the day after you shared the girls' spa day, but I had to put my own touch on it. I got it back from the jeweler three weeks ago, and it has killed me to not present it to you. If we didn't have this trip planned, I would have proposed. As it is, I was going to do it on the cruise Wednesday night, but I couldn't wait."

"I love that you couldn't wait." She throws her arms around my neck and her legs around my waist, our naked bodies fused under the water. We kiss, our tongues tangling with an air of desperation. "I'm not the most patient person either, you know."

"I know."

"For example... I'd love to throw the last of my birth control into the ocean." She bites her lip and smiles.

"You mean..." I arch my brow, letting her say what I've been thinking all along.

"Life is short. After the last year or so, we both know this. I don't want to wait years to start our family. We don't have to make ourselves crazy about it, but let's remove the one barrier keeping us from getting pregnant."

"Oh, angel. I can't wait to fill your belly with our child."

She reaches between us and strokes my length until I'm hard again. Honestly, it doesn't take much with her. "No better time than right now to start trying."

"I fucking love you."

"I love you more."

VETERAN
K9
TEAM
REPORTING
FOR DUTY

Second Epilogue
Bishop - Eight Months Later (Next Christmas)

"You know I'd do anything for you, but the first time you ask for a nine-foot Christmas tree is the day we start looking at single level ranchers." I lug the six-foot tree out of the elevator and follow Charity to our apartment. I'm sure the janitorial staff is going to be pissed when they come across the random pine needles in the lobby, but considering half the tenants have already brought their trees in, I figure they're used to cleaning them up.

"We need to start looking, anyway. We're about to outgrow this place." She rubs her hand over her small belly and stares out the windows at the world beyond.

She's four months along, and we just had our sixteen week checkup where we found out that we're having a boy—and yes, his name will be Chad.

I set down the Christmas tree and stop up behind her, sliding my hands around her waist. Pressing a kiss to her neck, I murmur in her ear, "I'll miss fucking you against these windows."

She gives me a bit of a sassy side eye. "We'll have to come up with other ways to exercise your exhibitionism."

I might have convinced her to stay naked ninety percent of the time we were in the Bahamas. She thinks I have a fetish, but really I just love having her naked and accessible.

"I don't need anyone seeing what I do to you but you." I bite her earlobe and then smack her ass, returning to the tree that needs to be stood up and watered.

As I manhandle the tree into the stand, Charity comes up and places a pitcher of water on the floor next to me. Then she sits down on the couch and watches, or more to the point, supervises my progress. Neither of us have many sentimental Christmas decorations, but what she doesn't know is that I got my hands on a box of ornaments her aunt had stashed away in the garage for the last five years, ever since her parents died. Couple these ornaments with a few from my parents, and the new ones we have with our wedding photo, and I'm thinking this is going to be a beautiful tree.

I cut the net keeping the unruly tree neatly bound and stand back as tree limbs fall into place. "How does it look?"

"It looks great."

"Hold that thought." I snag the net off the ground and run to the hall closet, pulling out two shoe boxes full of ornaments.

Taking a seat next to her, I put one box in her lap. "Merry Christmas, angel."

"What's this?"

"Open it and see."

She lifts the lid and her eyes grow wide, the ornament on top a picture of her and Chad as kids. "Oh my god, where did you get these?"

I slide my arm around her and pull her into my side. "At our reception your aunt mentioned she had some of your parents' stuff in her garage. A couple of weeks ago I went over to her house and dug through her crap until we found these."

Charity shakes her head, tears coming to her eyes. "I thought all of this was gone. I was away at college and Chad was in the field training when our parents died. My aunts and uncles organized the sale of the house for us, and honestly, I'd been too young at the time and in too much shock to think about stockpiling keepsakes."

"I think your aunt was waiting for you to have your own family."

Smiling, she turns and places her hands on my face. "And now I do."

Coming next: Karden and Sylvie in Mine to Protect

Most of my books take place in Spring City, Colorado

and feature cameo appearances from characters in past /
present / and sometimes future books from all of my
series. Check out my website for a cross-over /
series map.

Also by Kameron Claire

Want more **Witty** Tongues, **Wicked** Needs, & **Wild** Deeds?

Hollywood Lights (Pre-Order)

* Billionaire Romance *

Show Time (Securing Selyne)

Money Shot

Three Shot

Martini Shot

Long Shot

Veteran K9 Team

* *Military Romance* *

Mine to Cherish

Mine to Crave

Mine to Possess

Mine to Adore

Mine to Covet

Mine to Worship

Mine to Protect

Mine to Treasure

Hot Nights with the Boss

** Forbidden Office / Age-Gap Romances **

Dating the Boss

Flirting with the Boss

Teasing the Boss

Tempting the Boss

Rangers Football

** Sports Romance **

Play Action Fake

Quarterback Sneak

Personal Foul

Two-Point Conversion

Red Zone

Man to Man Coverage

Short Story Collections and Bundles

Animal Attraction 4-Story Collection

Vegas Nights 4-Story Collection

Last Stand Saloon 4-Story Collection

Instalove Bundle

Grayson Enterprises Series

Bedding the Boss

Enticing the Ex

Tempting the Teacher

Wedding the Widow

Exclusives and Sneak Peeks

Get exclusive stories, updates, sneak peeks, and special content only available to subscribers...

Join our Mailing List Today!

Sign Up Here

About the Author

USA Today Bestselling Author Kameron Claire writes stories with witty tongues, wicked needs, and wild deeds. Her books emphasize strong female leads and the protective alpha males who know how to love and support kick-ass, take-charge women. Many of her books contain military veterans, boss babes, gentle but dominant men, and goofy K9 hijinks.

Find her everywhere via linktr.ee/kameronclaire
Signed Paperbacks and discounted eBook bundles are available exclusively on her store
Subscribe to the Witty, Wicked & Wild community and read all her books online for as little as $5 a month.

www.ingramcontent.com/pod-product-compliance
Lightning Source LLC
Chambersburg PA
CBHW031625310726
48974CB00003B/825